An I Can Read Book™

MILDRED
and
SAM

by Sharleen Collicott

LAURA GERINGER BOOKS

An Imprint of HarperCollins*Publishers*

To my sister, Sharon, and Chuck Ferges,
who, like Mildred and Sam, prefer a house
that is big enough for their "visitors":
Doug, Michael, and Steven
—S.C.

HarperCollins®, 🐭®, and I Can Read Book® are
trademarks of HarperCollins Publishers Inc.

Mildred and Sam
Copyright © 2003 by Sharleen Collicott
Printed in the U.S.A. All rights reserved.
www.harperchildrens.com

Library of Congress Cataloging-in-Publication Data
Collicott, Sharleen.
    Mildred and Sam / by Sharleen Collicott.
        p.   cm.
    Summary: When eight baby mice arrive, their father finally understands why their mother
had wanted a bigger house.
    ISBN 0-06-026681-3 — ISBN 0-06-026682-1 (lib. bdg.) — ISBN 0-06-000200-X (pbk.)
    [1. Dwellings—Fiction.   2. Mice—Fiction.   3. Babies—Fiction.]   I. Title.
PZ7.C67758 Mi   2003   2001040369
[E]—dc21   CIP
                                                                                                AC

CONTENTS

HOUSE DREAMS

Mildred and Sam lived

in a tiny house

underneath the daffodil roots.

Sam was happy there.

Mildred was fidgety.

"There is no room for visitors,"

Mildred said.

"Visitors?"

Sam asked.

But Mildred only sighed.

One day, Mildred and Sam
climbed high in the old oak tree.
"Wouldn't it be nice to live here?"
asked Mildred.
"I like our house just fine,"
Sam said.
"There is plenty of room,"
said Mildred.
"True," Sam said.
"But there is no door
to keep us safe from the great owl."
Mildred only sighed.

That night, Mildred dreamed

that she and Sam lived

in the branches of the big oak tree.

In the dream, the great owl came

and carried them away.

They flew much too far from home.

So Mildred and Sam

had to make a fast escape.

The next day, Mildred and Sam
had a picnic on a lily pad.
"Wouldn't it be nice to live here?"
Mildred asked.
"I like our house just fine,"
Sam said.
"There is plenty of room,"
said Mildred.
"True," Sam said.
"But there is no door
to keep us safe from the things
that live at the bottom of the pond."
Mildred only sighed.

That night, Mildred dreamed

that she and Sam lived

on a great big lily pad.

In the dream, the frogs and fishes

took Mildred and Sam for a swim.

Down, down, down, they went.

It was much too deep.

So Mildred and Sam

had to make a fast escape.

The next day, Mildred and Sam

had tea and cookies

in the rose thicket.

"Wouldn't it be nice to live here?"

asked Mildred.

"I like our house just fine,"

Sam said.

"There is plenty of room,"

said Mildred.

"True," Sam said.

"But there is no door

to keep us safe from nosy bunnies."

Mildred only sighed.

That night, Mildred dreamed

that she and Sam lived

deep in the rose thicket.

In the dream,

an army of baby bunnies appeared

and stole all their cookies.

Finally, a mama bunny came

and scolded her babies.

While she was scolding,

Mildred and Sam decided

to make a fast escape.

The next day,

Sam got up extra early.

"I think it is time

to make you a bigger burrow,"

he told Mildred.

And he began to dig

underneath the daffodil roots.

The new house would have

plenty of room for visitors—

just in case.

GARDEN DREAMS

Sam worked on the new house,

but Mildred became fidgety again.

"Why don't you go visit your mother?"

Sam said.

But Mildred did not want to visit.

"Why don't you paint a picture?"

Sam asked.

But Mildred did not want to paint.

"I think I will plant a garden,"

she said at last.

So she ordered some seeds.

The next day, Mildred's seeds arrived.

Among the vegetable seeds

there was an unmarked packet.

"I did not order these!" Mildred said.

"Maybe they are special seeds,"

said Sam.

"Maybe something amazing will grow."

Mildred took one seed

from the unmarked packet

and planted it next to her carrots.

That night, Mildred dreamed

that she grew

a bushel of baby gourds.

"Hello, baby gourds," Mildred said.

She invited them all

into the new home Sam had built.

Inside the house,

the baby gourds sat on the furniture

and slept in the bed

and crowded around the kitchen table.

Even in the big new house,

there was no room

for Mildred and Sam.

"Mildred," Sam cried.

"When you said we might have visitors,

I did not think you meant

a bushel of baby gourds."

Mildred tried to round up the babies.

The little gourds

thought it was a game.

They all went running

out of the house.

"Eeeeeeeeeeeee!" they squealed.

Suddenly, two big gourds
came out of the woods.

"Our babies!" yelled Mama Gourd.

"See here, mouse,"
Papa Gourd said.

"That seed you planted
did not belong to you."

The big gourds marched off
back into the woods,
and their babies followed
close behind.

The next day, Mildred sent

the unmarked seeds back.

But first she made sure

she put a penny in the packet

to pay for the one seed she had planted.

As she watered her garden,

she looked at the ground.

She would have to wait and see

what her penny would bring.

Later that day, Mildred told Sam

she would help him with the house.

"I think we need an extra room,"

said Mildred.

"An extra room?"

Sam asked, scratching his head.

"I think the house

will be big enough."

"You never know," Mildred said.

MOUSE DREAMS

After the new house was all finished,
Sam was happy.

But Mildred was still fidgety.

Mildred remembered the oak tree
and the picnic.

She remembered the tea and cookies.

She got out her brushes
and began to paint.

She painted frogs and fish.

She painted bunnies and baby gourds.

She even painted the great white owl.

When Mildred was finished painting,

she began to sew.

She sewed blankets

out of roses and daffodils.

She even sewed slipcovers

out of lily pads.

When Mildred was finished sewing,

she began to knit.

She knitted tiny socks and pajamas.

She even knitted a big scarf for Sam.

When Mildred was finished knitting,

she began to bake.

She baked ginger-root muffins

and sunflower-seed pie.

She even made honeysuckle jam.

When Mildred was finished baking,

she finally settled down for a rest.

The very next day,

Mildred and Sam's new house

was filled with visitors—

eight tiny baby mice.

And the house was big enough

for all of them.